Pet Friends Forever

A No-Sneeze Pet

by Diana G. Gallagher

illustrated by Adriana Isabel Juárez Puglisi

Raintree is an imprint of Capstone Global Library Limited,
a company incorporated in England and Wales having its registered office at 7 Pilgrim
Street, London, EC4V 6LB - Registered company number: 6695582

www.raintreepublishers.co.uk
myorders@raintreepublishers.co.uk

Edited by Helen Cox Cannons
Designed by Kristi Carlson and Philippa Jenkins
Original illustrations © Capstone Global Library Ltd 2014
Image Credits: Shutterstock/Kudryashka (pattern)

Originated by Capstone Global Library Ltd
Production by Helen McCreath
Printed and bound in China

ISBN 978 1 406 27968 9
18 17 16 15 14
10 9 8 7 6 5 4 3 2 1

British Library Cataloguing in Publication Data
A full catalogue record for this book is available from the British Library.

TABLE OF CONTENTS

1

Emma's pet problem

Kyle sat on the steps, waiting for his best friend, Mia, to come over. Mia lived next door, and they almost always spent time together after school. Today they were taking Kyle's dog, Rex, to the park.

"Ruff!" Rex barked. The yellow Labrador retriever ran over and dropped a tennis ball at Kyle's feet.

"Do you want this?" Kyle asked, tossing the ball in the air. Rex caught it and brought it back. "Good boy!" He grinned and patted the dog's head.

Just then, Mia walked up. "Do you want to go for a W-A-L-K?" she asked, rubbing Rex behind his ears.

"Sure!" Kyle said. "Let's take R-E-X to the P-A-R-K."

They had to spell out *walk* and *park*. Rex knew what those words meant, and if he heard them, he wouldn't stop barking and jumping until they were on their way. Once Kyle hadn't been able to take him after he'd said he would, but Rex had kept barking and jumping until bedtime.

Kyle grabbed Rex's leash from the hook inside the front door and stuck it in his pocket so Rex wouldn't see. Then he and Mia ran over to his mum's office. Kyle's mum was a vet, and her office was right next door.

Lillian, the office manager and receptionist, was behind the reception counter when they pushed through the door.

"Hi, Lillian, is my mum busy at the moment?" Kyle asked.

"She has appointments until five," Lillian told him.

"Can you please tell Dr Blake that we're taking Rex to the park?" Mia asked.

"Of course," Lillian said. "Have fun."

"We will!" Kyle called over his shoulder as he and Mia ran back outside. Rex was still sitting on the porch with the ball between his paws, waiting for them.

Kyle pulled the leash out of his pocket and waved it in the air. "Park!" he called.

As soon as he saw the leash, Rex immediately started barking and spinning in happy circles.

Kyle grabbed the dog's collar. "Sit!" he said firmly.

Rex sat, but he didn't stop wiggling as Kyle snapped the leash onto his collar.

Mia laughed and picked up the ball. "Let's go!" she said.

The park was only two blocks away from where Kyle and Mia lived, so they usually walked there alone. Halfway there, they spotted Emma Peters, one of their classmates, sitting on her front porch. She waved to them as they walked past.

"Emma doesn't look very happy," Mia whispered to Kyle.

"Maybe she's just bored," Kyle said. "We should see if she wants to come with us."

Mia nodded. "Hey, Emma!" she called. "We're going to the park. Want to come?"

"Definitely!" Emma said happily. "Let me ask my mum." Emma disappeared inside the house. A few minutes later, she reappeared and bounded down the front steps to join them.

"Thanks for inviting me," Emma said as they continued on to the park. She looked at Rex nervously. "Does your dog bite?"

"No," Kyle said. "He's really nice. You can pet him if you want."

Emma shook her head. "That's okay," she said.

Kyle, Mia and Emma followed the signs to the fenced-off dog park area. As soon as they were inside the gate, Kyle took off Rex's leash, and Mia threw the ball. Rex immediately chased after it, brought it back, and dropped it at her feet.

"Wow! What other tricks does he do?" Emma asked.

"Watch." Kyle got Rex to sit, lie down, stay and come. Then he showed off the dog's other tricks. Rex shook hands, sat up on his haunches and caught a dozen sticks the children threw.

"He's so clever!" Emma exclaimed. "And he listens to you, too?"

"Unless he sees a squirrel," Kyle said with a laugh. "He never catches them, but he loves to try." There were only three things Rex liked better than chasing squirrels: playing ball, eating dog treats, and being with Kyle.

"Does he chew up stuff?" Emma asked.

"He ate some shoes when he was a puppy," Kyle said.

Emma's eyes got big. "Didn't your mum get mad?" she asked.

"Yeah, but she got over it," Kyle said. "Just like she got over the glasses I broke and the clothes I tore and the walls I coloured on."

"You coloured on the walls?" Emma asked.

"I was five," Kyle said, shrugging. "Now I know better."

"And so does Rex," Mia added. "He doesn't eat shoes or bury socks or bite chunks out of chair legs anymore."

"But he makes a huge mess if I forget to take out the rubbish," Kyle admitted. "He thinks ripping up papers and dragging rubbish all over the place is fun."

Emma made a face. "Having a dog sounds gross," she said.

Kyle shrugged. "Yeah, I guess the cleaning-up part is kind of gross," he agreed. "But taking out the rubbish is my job, and Rex is my dog. I have to do it."

Emma sighed. "I'd do it for my dog . . . if I had one," she said enviously.

The children were too busy talking to notice a squirrel scurrying across the dog park. But Rex noticed. The dog took off after it.

"Run, squirrel, run!" Mia yelled.

The squirrel scurried up a nearby tree. Rex barked and jumped, but the squirrel climbed out of reach. Then it dropped an acorn.

Bonk! The acorn smacked Rex right on the head. The dog barked one last time. Then he gave up and went looking for another squirrel to chase.

"He's so funny!" Emma laughed, but her smile quickly faded. "I wish I could have a dog."

"Why can't you?" Kyle and Mia asked at the same time.

"My mum is allergic to animal fur," Emma said. "That means no pets. Ever."

Mia gasped. "Oh, no!"

"Really?" Kyle asked. He couldn't imagine not having a pet. "Is that why you didn't want to pet Rex?"

"Yeah," Emma said with a sad sigh. "My mum's eyes get all red and watery, and she can't stop sneezing if she gets too close to a dog. Cats are worse. They make her itch."

Mia looked horrified. "I have a cat!" she exclaimed. "And she sheds."

"Well, I guess I shouldn't pet you either!" Emma joked.

Everyone laughed at her joke, but Emma's problem wasn't funny.

A no-sneeze idea

"I feel so bad for Emma," Kyle said. He and Mia were back at his house after their park outing.

"Me, too," Mia agreed. "I'd go crazy if my parents were allergic. I wouldn't be able to have Misty."

"And I wouldn't be able to have Rex," Kyle said. He stopped and gave Rex a big hug.

Kyle's mum treated all kinds of animals at her clinic, but he liked dogs the best. He couldn't imagine what his life would be like without his four-legged best friend. He just knew he'd be miserable.

"I love Misty so much," Mia said. "I don't even mind when she throws up hair balls on my bed."

"I know what you mean," Kyle said. "I don't mind cleaning up after Rex because I love him. Even when he tears the stuffing out of his dog toys and leaves it all over my room. He's my responsibility. I wish Emma could have a pet to love, too."

"I wish there was something we could do to help her," Mia added.

Kyle was quiet for a minute as he thought about the problem. Suddenly, an idea hit him. "I've got it!" he said. "Emma needs a no-sneeze pet! One that her mum won't be allergic to."

"That's a great idea!" Mia exclaimed. "Let's go ask your mum."

Dr Blake was in her office when Kyle and Mia walked into the clinic. She was finished seeing patients for the day, so it was okay to bring Rex inside. He immediately flopped down on the floor and closed his eyes.

Dr Blake reached down and patted the dog's head. "Did you have a hard day at the park, Rex?" she asked.

"He's probably tired from showing all his tricks to our friend Emma," Mia said.

"She can't have a dog because her mum is allergic to fur," Kyle added. "Can you believe that?"

"That's a shame," his mother said. "She could probably get allergy shots. A lot of people get those so they become less sensitive. But they can take years to work."

"Years?" Kyle exclaimed. "But Emma needs a pet now!"

"One that doesn't have fur," Mia added. "We thought you might have some good ideas."

"That's a great idea," Dr Blake said. "There are plenty of pets that wouldn't bother her mum's allergies."

Dr Blake made a list of pets that wouldn't bother Mrs Peters's allergies, including fish and reptiles such as snakes, iguanas and lizards. Then Kyle and Mia ran back to Emma's house to tell her about their idea for a no-sneeze pet.

"Hi!" Emma said, grinning at them as she opened the door. Then she frowned. "Where's Rex?"

"We left him at my mum's clinic so he wouldn't make your mum sneeze," Kyle said.

"We wanted to talk about your pet problem," Mia said.

"You need a pet that doesn't have fur," Kyle said.

"You mean like a turtle?" Emma asked.

"Something like that," Kyle said. He held up the list his mum had written. "My mum made a list of no-sneeze pets you could get!"

Emma looked hesitant. "I don't know if a no-sneeze pet would be the same," she said softly. "I really want a dog."

Just then Emma's mum walked up behind her. "You do?" she asked, looking surprised. "Why didn't you tell me?"

Emma looked down at the ground. "I didn't want you to feel bad," she said. "You can't help it if you're allergic."

"Oh, Emma," Mrs Peters said. She hugged her daughter and looked at Kyle and Mia. "Give us a minute, okay?"

Emma and her mum disappeared back inside the house. Kyle and Mia sat down on the step to wait. A moment later, Emma burst through the front door.

"She said yes!" Emma exclaimed. "I can have a no-sneeze pet."

"That's great news!" Kyle said. He and Mia grinned and high-fived each other happily.

Emma held up the list. "Now I just have to choose which one!"

3

Mr J's Pet Haven

The next day after school, Emma's mum drove Kyle, Mia, and Emma to Mr J's Pet Haven.

"I'll wait for you children here," Mrs Peters said as she parked the car. "That way I won't have to worry about my allergies."

"Okay," Emma said. "We'll be back." With that, she, Kyle and Mia all ran inside.

"Welcome!" a bright-green parrot called as the children opened the door. The colourful bird sat on a tall perch next to the front counter.

"Who's here, Jethro?" the man standing behind the counter asked. He peered at the children over the rim of his glasses.

"Hi, Mr J," Kyle said.

Mr Jabowski had opened his pet shop thirty years ago. Everyone called him Mr J. His shop didn't have as much stuff as some of the big chain stores, but he always remembered his customers and their pets. "Did Rex manage to destroy all his toys again?" Mr J asked.

"Not yet, but he's working on it," Kyle said. "We brought you a new customer."

"Hi, I'm Emma," Emma said.

Mr J squinted at Emma like he was thinking hard. "You look like a puppy person to me."

"I wish I was," Emma said. "But my mum's allergic. I need something without fur."

"Oh, I see," Mr J said, nodding. "That is a challenge." Then he clapped his hands together and smiled. "But I'm sure we can find a pet that's just right for you."

"I'm hungry!" Jethro screeched from his perch. Mr J gave the bird a piece of dried fruit.

"My mum made a list of pets Emma could have," Kyle said, holding up the paper. "Can you show us where the reptiles are? Emma's mum definitely won't be allergic to those."

"Of course!" Mr J said. "Follow me."

The shop owner led the children down one of the crowded aisles in the small shop. Both sides of the aisle were lined with snakes, lizards and turtles living in glass tanks. The turtles rested on a rock in a shallow bowl of water. The snakes and lizards had leaves to hide under and branches to climb on.

"They all look so creepy," Emma said. She shuddered. "I definitely don't want a reptile. Let's look at the birds."

Kyle glanced down at the paper in his hands. "Mum didn't put birds on the list," he said.

"That's weird," Emma said. "They don't have fur."

The three children followed Mr J over to a separate room where the birds were kept. He had yellow and orange canaries, blue and green parakeets, tiny finches and a grey parrot.

Emma walked up to the parrot. "Does this parrot talk like Jethro does?" she asked.

Mr J shook his head. "It takes a long time to teach parrots to talk," he explained. "I've had Jethro for twenty-five years. He learnt most of his words from my children."

"Wow!" Kyle said. "Twenty-five years? That's longer than we've been alive!"

Mr J laughed. "Some parrots can live for more than fifty years," he told them.

Emma looked a little nervous. "That's a really long time," she said. "Maybe we should look at something else."

They moved out of the room and walked past a line of cages holding guinea pigs, gerbils and hamsters.

"Oh, they're all so cute!" Mia exclaimed. "And tiny!"

"They might be cute and tiny, but they all have fur," Emma said, shaking her head sadly. "I don't think these will work either."

"How about fish?" Mr J suggested. "They don't have fur."

"And they're on the list!" Kyle added happily.

Emma shrugged. "I guess it's worth a try," she said.

The group headed for the back of the shop where three rows of 38-litre glass tanks lined the wall. Ceramic decorations, colourful rocks, and a variety of plastic plants were stored underneath. Aquarium kits, tank supplies, and stands were displayed in the corner.

"Wow!" Emma exclaimed. "I didn't know there were so many different kinds of tropical fish."

Suddenly a bell chimed and Jethro squawked, "Hello!" from the front of the shop.

"Sounds like I've got another customer," Mr J said. "I'd better go see who it is. You children keep looking."

Mr J headed back to the front of the shop. Kyle, Mia and Emma stayed back and studied the colourful fish.

"They're all pretty," Mia said. "Except for the catfish. They're pretty ugly."

"But they keep the tank clean," a voice said from behind them.

A teenage girl walked over. She was carrying a mouse-shaped toy and a bag of cat treats. "Do you have a fish tank?" Kyle asked.

"I used to, but it was really hard to keep clean," the girl said. "Catfish eat the algae that grows on the glass, but they don't eat everything. I had to take the whole tank apart to rinse the rocks."

"Is that why you don't have an aquarium now?" Emma asked.

The girl nodded. "It was too much work," she said. "I gave them away and got a cat instead. It's still work, but at least I can cuddle my cat."

"I can't have a cat," Emma said sadly. "My mum is allergic."

"Oh, no!" the girl said. "Well, good luck. I'm sure you'll find something." With that, she headed off to pay for her purchases.

"I don't think I want fish," Emma said.

"Too much work?" Kyle asked.

"Fish are pretty, but you can't cuddle them," Emma said.

Kyle frowned. "None of the no-sneeze pets on the list are cute or cuddly," he said. "But that doesn't mean that they can't be cuddled. I mean, that boy at school walked around with a toad in his shirt pocket all last summer!"

"Ew!" Mia said, shuddering. "That was so gross."

"I want a pet, but I can't decide which one," Emma said, sounding discouraged. "What if I never find one?"

Kyle and Mia sighed. Even a trip to the pet shop wasn't solving Emma's pet problem.

The scaredy snake

At school the next day, Kyle, Mia, and Emma asked all their friends and classmates about their pets. They thought it might be easier for Emma to decide which pet was right for her if she had a chance to see them at their owners' homes.

"Why do you want to know?" Lucy Owens asked.

Kyle explained Emma's pet problem. "She can't decide what to get," he said. "We thought it might help to visit people who have reptiles or birds."

"My brother has a pet snake," Lucy offered. "You can come and see it after school if you want."

Emma looked a little doubtful, but she nodded anyway. "I guess it couldn't hurt," she said.

That afternoon, Kyle, Mia and Emma walked to Lucy's house. Her brother, Tommy, was in Year 8, but he didn't act too cool to talk to the younger children. He was proud of his snake and wanted to show off.

"I call him the Great Gorgon," Tommy said, showing them to the glass tank where he kept his snake. There was a screen top taped to the glass tank. Tommy ripped off the tape, took off the top and picked up the snake.

"What kind of snake is it?" Emma asked.

"He's a ball python," Tommy said as the reptile curled around his arm.

"A python!" Emma exclaimed. "They get gigantic!"

"Burmese pythons get huge, but ball pythons only grow to just over a metre long," Tommy explained. "Want to touch him?"

Emma shook her head. "I don't think so," she said quickly.

Mia reached out and ran her finger over the reptile's skin. "He's not slimy," she said, sounding surprised.

Emma tentatively touched the snake, but quickly yanked her hand back when the Great Gorgon moved.

"He won't hurt you," Tommy reassured her. He uncoiled the snake from his arm and held it out to Emma. "Here. Hold him."

"Aghh!" she screamed.

Her loud screech startled the Great Gorgon. The snake hissed and coiled into a ball in Tommy's hands.

"That snake is a sissy," Kyle said with a laugh.

"That's why they're called ball pythons," Tommy explained. "They curl up and hide their heads when they're scared."

"I scared him?" Emma asked, looking surprised.

"Everything scares him," Tommy said. "I thought naming him something tough would make him braver, but it didn't work."

"I'm sorry, snake," Emma said. She gently stroked the snake's back. "You're not so bad."

Tommy put the Great Gorgon back in his tank. He used new tape to keep the screen lid on and pressed it down firmly.

"Does the tape keep him from getting out?" Mia asked.

"Most of the time," Tommy said. "He's a wimp, but he's also a great escape artist. Most snakes are."

Emma shuddered. "I don't want to have nightmares about loose snakes in my room!" she said. "I don't think a snake is the right pet for me either."

Kyle, Mia and Emma thanked Tommy for showing them his pet snake and headed for the front door.

"Now what?" Emma asked.

"Well, snakes are out and so are fish," Mia said. "What else is on the no-sneeze pet list?"

Lucy thought for a minute. "I know!" she said. "You have to visit the Bird Lady!"

5

A flurry of feathers

The Bird Lady was a woman called Mrs
Milton. She lived next door to Lucy. Kyle knew
who she was because whenever Mrs Milton
needed a vet, she brought her birds to Dr
Blake's clinic. He'd seen her in there plenty of
times.

"Hello, everyone!" Mrs Milton said when
they knocked on her door.

"Thanks for letting us come over to see your birds," Kyle said.

"No problem," Mrs Milton replied. "I'm happy to show them off."

"This is Emma," Mia said. "She's trying to decide what type of animal to get as a pet. That's why we wanted to see your birds."

"It's nice to meet you, dear," Mrs Milton said. "I'm glad you're thinking about a bird. Birds make fabulous pets!"

"Does your bird talk like Mr J's parrot, Jethro?" Emma asked.

Mrs Milton laughed. "I wish Deedle Dum talked as well as Jethro does," she said. "He certainly tells you what he's thinking, though."

Mrs Milton led Kyle, Mia and Emma into the kitchen. A large birdcage sat in the corner. Inside was a beautiful grey parrot. Deedle Dum wasn't as big as Jethro, but he had a bigger perch.

"Get lost!" the parrot screeched as they walked into the kitchen. Kyle and the girls giggled.

Mrs Milton shook her head. "Deedle Dum, be nice! He said that when I got him," she explained to the children. "I don't think his last owner was very friendly."

"Does he say anything else?" Emma asked.

"Shut up!" the bird squawked, ruffling his feathers.

"And he bites," Mrs Milton said.

"But you love him anyway, right?" Kyle asked.

"Of course! Nobody else would," Mrs Milton joked. "Let me show you the rest of my birds."

Kyle, Mia and Emma followed Mrs Milton. The tweets, chirps and squawks got louder when they left the kitchen. There were caged birds in every room. Mrs Milton had more finches, canaries and parakeets than Mr J's Pet Haven!

They came to a stop in front of a cage full of beautiful yellow canaries. "What do you think?" Mia asked Emma.

"I love the way the canaries sing, and the finches are adorable," Emma said. "But I think the parakeets have more personality. They're like parrots, except smaller."

"What's in that room?" Kyle asked, pointing to a closed door down the hall.

"That's my bird hospital," Mrs Milton said. She opened the door so they could peek inside. "I only have two patients at the moment. There's a raven with a broken wing and a blue jay with missing tail feathers."

"Oh, I remember the raven," Kyle said. "Mum put the splint on his wing when you found him."

"Will they ever be able to fly again?" Mia asked.

"I hope so," Mrs Milton said. "We'll have to wait and see."

"Why do you have so many birds?" Emma asked.

"I take birds that people don't want anymore, like Deedle Dum," Mrs Milton explained. "Some people don't think things through before they decide to get a pet. Then they realize after the fact that they can't handle the responsibility." She smiled at Emma. "I'm glad you're taking the time to find the right pet for you before you make a mistake."

"I really want a dog," Emma said. "But my mum is allergic. So I have to get a no-sneeze pet. I really like birds!"

Mrs Milton's bright smile faded. "Oh, no," she said. "I'm afraid you can't have a bird, then. Their feathers carry allergens just like fur."

Kyle sighed. "No wonder birds aren't on the list," he said. "I thought my mum just forgot."

Emma's face crumpled. "I'm never going to get a pet, am I?" she asked sadly.

6

The banana beast

Dr Blake's clinic was closed on Saturday afternoons, so Kyle's mum had volunteered to take Kyle, Mia and Emma to visit another no-sneeze pet.

"You two are awfully quiet today," Dr Blake told Kyle and Mia as she pulled out of the driveway. "Is something wrong? Do you want to talk about it?"

"I just don't know what to do," Mia explained. She shook her head unhappily. "Emma hasn't found a pet she likes, and Charley is the last one on the list."

Kyle shook his head. "I don't think she's going to like him," he said.

"Let's allow Emma to decide for herself," Dr Blake said.

Emma was waiting for them on her front porch when they pulled up. She hurried to the car and hopped in the back seat with Mia and Kyle.

"No luck finding a pet yet, Emma?" Dr Blake asked. "What was wrong with the other pets on the list?"

"Fish just swim around," Emma explained. "They're kind of boring. And they don't live very long. And snakes can get loose and they eat mice. I liked Mrs Milton's birds, but bird feathers carry allergens like fur."

"You won't have to worry about today's pet eating mice," Mia said. "Mr Bernard's pet is a vegetarian. He'll live a long time, too."

"And Charley is definitely not boring," Kyle added.

"What kind of pet is it?" Emma asked.

"You'll see," Kyle said.

"We're here!" Dr Blake announced. She pulled into a driveway and everyone hopped out of the car.

There was an older man waiting for them on the front porch.

"Emma, this is Mr Bernard," Dr Blake said. "He's been bringing Charley to my clinic for years."

"Nice to meet you, Emma," Mr Bernard said. "Dr Blake tells me you're looking for a pet that won't bother your mum's allergies."

Emma nodded.

"I hope meeting Charley will help. Come on in, everyone," Mr Bernard said.

As they followed him into the house, Kyle turned to Emma. "Now, don't freak out," he warned her. "Charley isn't as scary as he looks."

"Scary? What is he?" Emma asked.

"He's a–" Mia started to say.

"Dragon!" Emma squealed when she caught sight of the enormous lizard lounging on Mr Bernard's living-room sofa.

Dr Blake laughed. "Close," she said. "Charley is an iguana."

"He looks a little like a dragon, though," Mr Bernard added. The bright-green iguana was 1.5 metres long from his nose to the tip of his tail, and he weighed 5.4 kilograms.

Kyle grinned. "Don't worry, I freaked out a little the first time I met Charley, too," he said.

"Are all iguanas as big as Charley?" Emma asked.

Mr Bernard shook his head. "He was only this big when I got him ten years ago," he said, holding his hands about 30 centimetres apart.

"You've had him for ten years?" Emma asked. "That's a long time."

"He could live to be twenty," Dr Blake told Emma.

"Will he get twice as big as he is now?" Emma asked.

"I hope not! If he does, I'll have to move out!" Mr Bernard joked.

But Emma didn't laugh. She glanced over at the cage in the corner. "How did he get out of his cage?" she asked nervously. "Did he escape?"

"No, I let him run loose in the house," Mr Bernard said. "Except when my sister comes to visit. Then I lock him up. She thinks he's icky."

"He looks mean," Emma said.

"Iguanas aren't mean," Dr Blake said. "But you do have to be careful, just like with any pet. Iguanas can bite and whip their tails if they think they're in danger or scared."

"He scares me!" Emma exclaimed.

"Not me," Mia said, reaching out to gently rub Charley's head. "I've seen Charley plenty of times at Dr Blake's office. See? He's sweet."

Charley, however, wasn't in the mood for company. He hissed, jumped off the sofa, and stared down the intruders.

Emma hid behind Kyle. "Why is he bobbing his head like that?" she exclaimed. "Is he going to attack?"

"No, he wants a treat," Mr Bernard said as he headed for the kitchen. Charley instantly turned away from his guests and followed his owner out of the room.

Just then, Dr Blake's mobile phone rang. "You lot go ahead," she said. "I have to answer this."

Kyle, Mia and Emma headed into the kitchen. Charley was strutting back and forth as Mr Bernard peeled a banana. He knelt down and held it out to Charley. The iguana immediately opened his mouth wide and mashed the end off.

"He really likes bananas," Mia said.

"More than anything." Mr Bernard said. He dropped the half-eaten fruit onto the floor.

"Charley is kind of cool," Emma admitted, "but I want a pet I can hug." She sighed sadly. "I guess there's no such thing for a child whose mum is allergic to furry animals."

"Hold on a second," Mr Bernard said. "That's not exactly true."

An almost-perfect pet

"What do you mean?" Kyle asked, looking confused. "Fur is fur, right?"

"Not always," Mr Bernard said with a grin. "My six-year-old grandson is allergic, just like Emma's mum. But his sister has a furry pet."

"She does?" Emma exclaimed. Her eyes lit up with excitement.

"Are you serious?" Kyle asked. He rechecked the no-sneeze list. There were no furry animals.

"Of course!" Mr Bernard said. "Katie and Karl live right next door. I'll give them a call and see if you can come over."

Kyle, Mia and Emma went outside to wait.

"I bet she has a stuffed animal for a pet," Mia whispered with a giggle.

"Or one of those robot dogs," Kyle suggested.

"I hope not," Emma said, crossing her fingers for good luck. "I want a real, live pet I can cuddle!"

Dr Blake was finishing up her phone call when the children walked onto the porch.

"Do you have an emergency?" Kyle asked his mum. She was always available if something bad happened to one of her patients, even in the middle of the night.

Dr Blake shook her head and smiled. "No, your dad couldn't find the furniture polish," she said with a laugh.

A few minutes later, Mr Bernard walked out onto the porch. "My daughter said it's fine for you to go over," he said. "Katie would love to show you her pet."

The whole group walked next door. A girl around Kyle, Mia and Emma's age answered the front door.

"Hi, Grandpa," she said, giving Mr Bernard a hug.

"Hi, Katie," he replied with a smile. "These are the children I was telling you about. Emma is looking for a pet that won't bother her mum's allergies."

"Do you really have a no-sneeze pet with fur?" Emma asked. She looked at Katie hopefully.

Katie nodded happily. "I certainly do! His name is Duke," she said. "He's the best! Come on, I'll show you!"

Kyle, Mia and Emma followed Katie to her bedroom. Dr Blake stayed behind to chat with Mr Bernard and Katie's mum.

"Where's Duke?" Emma asked when they reached Katie's room.

"In here," Katie said. She walked over to a glass cage on her dresser. The bottom of the cage was covered with wood shavings and shredded paper.

Kyle peered inside. There was a food dish, a plastic wheel, and a pile of chew sticks. A water bottle was attached to the side of the cage. Duke ran out of a little wicker basket that looked like an upside-down bowl with a hole in the side.

"A hamster!" Emma exclaimed. "He's so adorable!"

Duke sat up on his haunches, watching them and twitching his nose. His cheeks were puffed out, and he used his little paws to rub his face.

"Does he just look cute or can he do tricks and stuff, too?" Kyle asked.

"He doesn't do tricks, but he does lots of other things," Katie said. She took the hamster out of his cage and put him into a green, plastic ball. "He runs in his wheel, and he loves to roll around in his ball. I put him in there when I have to clean the cage."

"Look at him go!" Emma exclaimed as Duke took off across the room. When the ball hit the wall, he turned and rolled the other way.

"I'm saving my money to get him one of those plastic playhouses," Katie said. "Hamsters love crawling around in the tubes and cubbies."

"Can you hold him?" Emma asked.

"Of course!" Katie said. She took Duke out of his ball and set him on her shoulder. The hamster immediately burrowed closer, and Katie giggled. "He likes to snuggle in my hair, but it tickles!"

"That's sort of like a hug," Mia told Emma.

"You can hug him if you want," Katie offered. She reached out and put Duke in Emma's hands.

Emma gently held the little animal up to her cheek. "I love him!" she exclaimed.

Kyle didn't want to be the bad guy, but he had to ask. "But hamsters have fur," he pointed out. "So why doesn't Duke make your brother sneeze?"

"Probably because they're so tiny that they don't have a lot of fur," Katie said. "Duke stays in my room, and I keep his cage clean. Plus I vacuum in here every day."

Kyle looked at Mia. "I think we've done it! I think we've found the perfect no-sneeze pet for Emma!"

"Now we just have to make sure it's okay with my mum," Emma said. Suddenly, she looked worried again.

The hamster project

Dr Blake dropped Kyle, Mia and Emma off at Emma's house to talk to her mum about their solution to the pet problem. They found Mrs Peters in her back garden.

"Hey, Mum," Emma said. "Can I talk to you? I have something important to ask."

"Of course. What is it?" Emma's mum asked. She stopped digging and gave Emma her full attention.

Emma looked nervous. "We were just over at a friend's house, and her brother is allergic to fur, but she has a hamster and it's so small it doesn't make him sneeze, so can I get one?" she asked without taking a breath.

Kyle and Mia had coached Emma in the car on what to say. She had several guaranteed-to-convince-an-adult arguments: Pets teach children to be responsible. Pets keep children company. Pets help children learn to respect the feelings of others.

Emma went for honesty instead. "I really, really want a pet to love," she said. "I can't have a dog, and you wouldn't want a giant lizard or a snake slithering around," she said. "A hamster won't make you itch or sneeze if I keep it in my room. It's like the perfect pet!"

"It certainly sounds like it," Emma's mum said. "And it sounds like you've put a lot of work and thought into this."

"I have," Emma said, nodding eagerly.

"Okay," Mrs Peters said.

"Okay?" Emma repeated. Her eyes grew wide. "Is that a yes?"

"That's a yes," her mum answered with a smile.

Emma squealed with excitement. "Thank you, Mum!" she cried. She turned to Kyle and Mia and hugged them both. "And thank you both, too! I couldn't have found the perfect no-sneeze pet without your help."

Mrs Peters agreed to take Kyle, Mia and Emma to Mr J's Pet Haven that afternoon. Emma wanted to pick out her no-sneeze pet right away.

Mr J greeted them at the front door. "Back again?" he asked. "Did you work out which pet is right for you?"

"I'm getting a hamster," Emma told him happily. "They're cute and cuddly and won't make my mum sneeze."

"Great choice!" Mr J said. "I have lots of different hamsters for you to choose from."

Emma, Kyle, Mia and Mrs Peters followed Mr J towards the front of the shop. "Mine!" Jethro squawked at the group as they got closer. "What's up?"

"Jethro learnt to talk from Mr J's children," Emma explained to her mum. "He's a lot nicer than Mrs Milton's parrot."

"Hamsters don't talk, do they?" Mrs Peters teased.

"Only at night when they think no one is listening," Mr J replied. He winked at Emma. "Last night they had a big argument."

Emma giggled and played along. "What were they fighting about?" she asked.

"Which one was going home with you today!" Mr J said with a grin.

"Who won?" Kyle asked.

"We won't know until Emma picks one," Mr J said.

The shop owner helped Emma and her mum choose a cage with a food dish and a water bottle. They added a plastic wheel, a ball and a wicker hamster house.

"Don't forget chew sticks," Mr J said. "Hamsters need to chew on something to keep their teeth from growing too long. Chew sticks will keep him from chewing on his cage.

When they'd gathered all the necessary supplies, they headed over to the hamster area. All the hamsters were in separate cages. Most of them were taking naps.

"Do hamsters sleep all the time?" Emma asked.

"Hamsters are nocturnal," Mr J said. "They like to sleep during the day."

Emma grinned. "That's perfect! He'll want to play at night when I'm not at school."

"I think that one likes you," Mrs Peters said, pointing to a white hamster that had wiggled out of his plastic house. The hamster sat up, looked straight at Emma and wiggled his nose.

Emma pointed right at it. "That's the one I want," she said without hesitation.

Kyle read the sign on the cage. "It says he's a Winter White dwarf hamster," he read aloud.

"I'm going to call him Bernie," Emma said, "because Mr Bernard told us about hamsters. I hope he doesn't mind."

"I think Mr Bernard will be honoured," Emma's mum said.

After Mrs Peters paid for everything, Kyle and Mia went back to Emma's house to help get Bernie settled. They went straight to Emma's bedroom and closed the door. The hamster was in a little box with air holes, but Emma wasn't taking any chances. She didn't want him to escape.

They set up his cage with the bedding on the bottom and the hamster house in one corner. Emma attached the water bottle to the side of the cage. When the cage was ready, they left Bernie alone to get used to his new home. It was time for Kyle and Mia to head home anyway. They had to feed their own pets.

"How's Bernie doing?" Mrs Peters asked when they walked through the kitchen. She was adding a powder to a pot on the hob.

"He's so cute and cuddly," Emma said. "I love him so much."

"I'm so glad–" Emma's mum paused. Then she sneezed. "Ah-choo!"

Kyle, Mia and Emma froze.

"Oh, no!" Emma cried. "You're allergic to my hamster!"

"What?" Mrs Peters looked stunned. Then she laughed. "No, I'm not. I'm making chilli, and I got pepper in my nose!"

Emma let out a sigh of relief. "Phew!" she said.

Emma walked them to the front door and let them out. Kyle and Mia waved and headed down the street.

"I'm glad we finally found Emma the perfect no-sneeze pet," Mia said as they headed for their own homes. "But I'm also glad the hunt is over."

"Me, too," Kyle said. "Now I'll have more time to play with Rex! He'll always be my favourite. Even if he isn't a no-sneeze pet!"

AUTHOR BIO

Diana G. Gallagher lives in Florida, USA, with three dogs, eight cats and a cranky parrot. She has written more than 90 books. When she's not writing, Gallagher likes gardening, garage sales and spending time with her grandchildren.

ILLUSTRATOR BIO

Adriana Isabel Juárez Puglisi has been a freelance illustrator and writer for more than twenty years and loves telling stories. She currently lives in Granada, Spain, with her husband, son, daughter, two dogs, a little bird and several fish.

GLOSSARY

algae (AL-gee) — small plants without roots or stems that grow in water or on damp surfaces

allergic (uh-LUR-jik) — if you are allergic to something, it causes you to sneeze, develop a rash, or have another unpleasant reaction

challenge (CHAL-uhnj) — something difficult that requires extra work or effort to do

miserable (MIZ-ur-uh-buhl) — sad, unhappy, or dejected

sensitive (SEN-suh-tiv) — easily offended or hurt; painful

separate (SEP-uh-rate) — different, individual, or not together

CARING FOR YOUR PET HAMSTER

Hamsters can make great pets. They are small animals and don't take up much space, so they're good if you don't have a lot of room. Hamsters are fun and friendly animals, but like any pet, they need to be taken care of. Here are some tips for caring for your hamster!

- Hamsters need a cage to live in. A good cage should have a deep, plastic base, a wire top, and different levels for your hamster to move around.

- Hamsters also need a separate area in their cage to sleep. This is called a nesting box.

- Wood shavings are the best bedding to use. Don't use pine or cedar shavings since they can make hamsters very ill.

- Hamsters love cardboard tubes. They run through them like they would tunnels in the wild.

- Hamsters need plenty of exercise and should be able to move around their cage. You can also put a wheel in your hamster's cage so it can run!

- Your hamster should always have a fresh supply of clean water. A water-dropper bottle is the best way to give water.

DISCUSSION QUESTIONS

1. Kyle and Mia both love animals, epecially their own pets. Do you have a pet? Talk about what makes your pet special. If you don't have a pet, talk about one you'd like to have.

2. Do you know anyone with allergies like Emma's mum? Talk about how they deal with animals.

3. If you had to choose a no-sneeze pet like Emma, which one would you have picked? Talk about your choice.

WRITING PROMPTS

1. Kyle and Mia are best friends. Write a paragraph about your best friend. How did you meet? What types of things do you like to do together?

2. Kyle's mum works with animals every day in her job as a vet. Write a paragraph about what you want to do when you're an adult.

3. Write about some other ways Kyle and Mia could have helped Emma solve her pet problem.